THE ROYAL BAKE OFF

Clémentine Beauvais

Illustrated by Becka Moor

BLOOMSBURY

LONDON OXFORD NEW YORK NEW DELHI SYDNEY

The story so far …

BRITLAND BLATHER

'PRINCE PEPINO FOUND AFTER THREE DAYS OF FRANCIAN WANDERINGS'

The heir to the throne of Britland, Prince Pepino, has been found again after disappearing for three days.

'We bumped into Pepino at the wedding of Princess Violette of Francia,' said Queen Sheila. 'He'd been to Parii with his friends without telling us, the cheeky little monkey!'

The prince and his two friends, Holly and Anna Burnbright, reportedly worked in Parii for Francian

Royal Wedding organiser Mademoiselle Malypense. It's been a busy week for the three children, who last Monday repelled the invasion of Britland by King Alaspooryorick of Daneland.

The Royal Family of Britland was attending the wedding of Violette of Francia to King Dentu of

Romany, although the Francian Princess changed her mind at the last minute and married a non-royal she was actually in love with.

'Young princesses these days,' sighed Queen Sheila. 'They think they need to be in love to get married! When in fact it's all a matter of how well your future spouse plays table football.'

It is believed that the three children are trying to earn money to go on the Holy Moly Holiday advertised in all the Britland newspapers. Anna Burnbright stated: 'We're looking for another summer job, since we didn't get paid for that one.' Let's hope for the sake of those greedy young girls that the next job pays a little more than that.

Chapter One

There is nothing quite so bothersome as badly combed seaweed, especially when it's growing on a pile of rocks on the beach outside the windows of your royal palace. Thus Queen Sheila and King Steve of Britland, one sunny summer morning after returning from Francia, asked Prince Pepino and Holly and Anna Burnbright to work as rock hairdressers for the day.

‘Just make them look pretty,’ said Queen Sheila. ‘We’ll reward you, of course. You’ll each get a new island named after you.’

‘Can we have real money instead?’ asked Anna.

‘What a disgusting request!’ King Steve exclaimed. ‘What do you need money for?’

‘A holiday we saw advertised in the newspaper,’ said Anna.

They had explained this to the King and Queen many times, but they kept forgetting. That holiday was called the Holy Moly Holiday, and it sounded like the absolute best experience of a lifetime. It was also very expensive.

HOLY MOLY HOLIDAY!

This summer, treat yourself to the intergalactic holiday of a lifetime – Not for the faint-hearted or the unadventurous!

DAY 1: Scuba-dive in the molten lava of the Eyjafjallajökull volcano of Islandia!

DAY 2: Learn to play polo on baby-elephant-back in the savannahs of Afrik!

DAY 3: Build a faster-than-light spaceship in Americanada!

DAY 4: Fly the faster-than-light spaceship to Mars, and have Martian cocktails at a local bar!

DAY 5: Back to Earth! Have a rest and celebrate the end of your Holy Moly Holiday in your ...

TEN STAR HOTEL!

With:

* Taps of hot chocolate, lemonade and chicken soup (unlimited)
* Marshmallow pillows (unlimited)
* Jacuzzi in every room (the size of an Olympic swimming pool)
* TV with three million channels (none of them boring)
* And much more ... including a

BIG, SECRET, SURPRISE GIFT!

'Why can't you ask your parents for money?' asked King Steve.

'We only have our mum, and she's poor,' said Holly. Their dad had disappeared years ago in the beak of a pelican. (That sort of thing is unlucky, but happens rarely enough that one shouldn't worry too much about it in everyday life.) 'She's a writer of ABC books, and there isn't much she can do to get paid more: A is always worth one pound and B another pound, and she's never allowed to add more letters to the alphabet.'

'We will pay you one pound per rock,' said King Steve. 'And I will pass a new law adding two letters to the alphabet. Or even three.'

'It might be c*mplΔcat~d,' said Queen Sheila, 'but all right, dear, if you wish.'

Prince Pepino, Holly and Anna started their job immediately, armed with a new rock hairdressing kit.

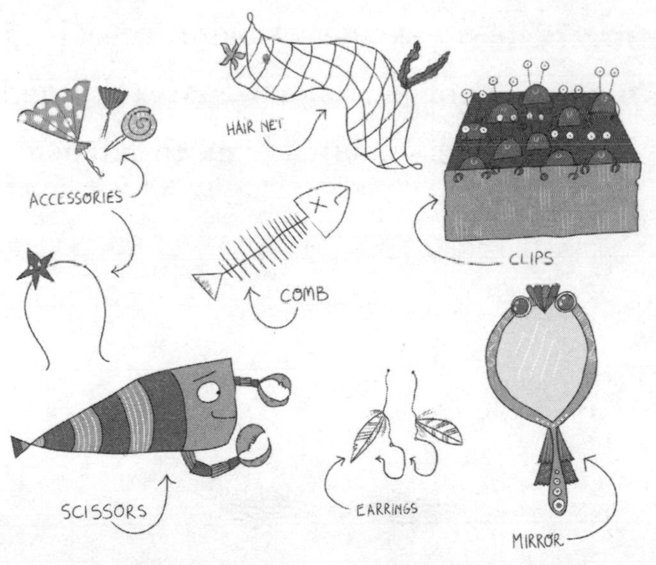

They soon realised that the job wasn't going to be easy. The brown seaweed was too rubbery to be plaited, and the green seaweed was full of sand mites.

'That's the tenth crab that refuses to be clipped at the end of a braid!' Anna cursed.

'And I'm having trouble with those anemones,' Holly complained. 'They keep squirting seawater on me when I try to cut that rock's fringe.'

'You're just not very talented,' said Prince Pepino. 'My rocks are already much prettier.'

Anna threw away the crab, which stuck its tongue out at her. 'I feel,' she said, 'like my life is spent working, working, working, with no deeper meaning at all.'

'I know,' said Pepino sadly. 'It happens to me

when I've been learning times tables for three minutes. I just want to scr–'

'AAAAAAAAAAAAAHHHHHHHHHHHH!'

The three children looked up at the palace. That high-pitched scream could only have come from one moustachioed mouth: King Steve's.

'What's wrong, Dad?' Pepino shouted up. 'Did you step on one of the Berties' pet centipedes again?'

The King appeared at the window, looking as pale as a frog's belly. 'I've just had *my brother* on the phone,' he said.

'Poor Daddy,' whispered Pepino. 'Let's go back to the palace. He'll need to be fed marshmallows through a tube.'

King Steve was lying on his bed eating flapjacks, cookies, peanut butter cups and, of course, marshmallows. The Queen was fanning him with a cloud of candyfloss, which King Steve stuffed in his mouth as the children walked in.

'My darling,' said the Queen, 'what can Sam possibly have said to make you so distressed?'

'Uncle Sam,' Pepino explained quietly to Holly and Anna, 'is the Emperor of Americanada. He married the Empress, but she's always abroad with her army, so he basically rules the country on his own. The biggest, richest country in the world! It makes Dad a little bit jealous.'

'Jealous!' sniffled King Steve, blowing his nose in the royal bedcovers. 'I'm not *jealous* of my brother! I don't care that he's richer than me, and more handsome and successful! I don't even care that he's decided to – to start *baking*!'

'*Baking*!' the Queen exclaimed. 'Oh, Stevie darling! Don't tell me –'

'That's right! The ONLY THING I do well – he *had* to try it too! And of course he does it *seriously* now – he's taking *classes*. He's already won competitions in Americanada!'

Queen Sheila tut-tutted. The King, having run out of bedcovers, attempted to blow his nose into the fur of one of their angora kittens (the kitten bit his chin).

'And of course,' said King Steve, 'it's not

enough for Sam. He must show *me* that he's the best at it. He's organising a *Royal Bake Off* – and he wants me to be a contestant!'

'Oh, you'll win easily, Daddy,' said Pepino. 'You're the best-ever cake maker. Remember when you won the South-East Britland Crab-Apple Crumble Competition? Look, the picture's still on the wall!'

'Crab-apple crumbles!' King Steve snorted. 'Look at the picture Sam's sent me on the Visiophone. He's just finished making a life-sized nougat and praline *skyscraper*. A hundred floors! With energy-drink-powered lifts! Of course his people adore him.'

'Your people adore you too,' said Queen Sheila. 'The newspapers keep saying how much of a laugh you are.'

'That's because they laugh *at* me!' moaned King Steve. 'You think I didn't read today's news story mocking me because I still can't count to ten? I've read it one, two, three, eight, four, five, nine, six, eight, ten times! I've had enough. I will take up his challenge – I will take part in the Royal Bake Off!'

'Oh, Steve – we're all so proud of you!' the Queen stammered, a bit tearful.

'I need to find some assistants,' said the King. 'Sam mentioned that each contestant could bring up to three kitchen helpers, who would be paid five hundred pounds each. The only condition is that they should have no baking experience whatsoever. Where could I find people like that?'

'*Ahem*,' coughed Anna. '*Ahem*, *ahem*, *ahem!*'

'*Ahem!*' coughed Holly. '*Ahem!*'

After ten or so minutes of coughing, the Queen, King and prince understood what they were alluding to – and King Steve phoned his brother to roar, 'I'm coming, Sam! And with the three most unqualified assistants in the world!'

Chapter Two

The next day, Holly and Anna arrived at the Royal Palace Airport early with tidy little suitcases. Prince Pepino and King Steve's suitcases were a bit less tidy.

'It's going to take a while to go through airport security,' Holly murmured.

Especially as the King and Pepino spent some time sliding into the X-ray machine and laughing at pictures of their skeletons.

'Look!' said Pepino. 'That must be the apricot stone I swallowed last summer. It's growing into a proper tree!'

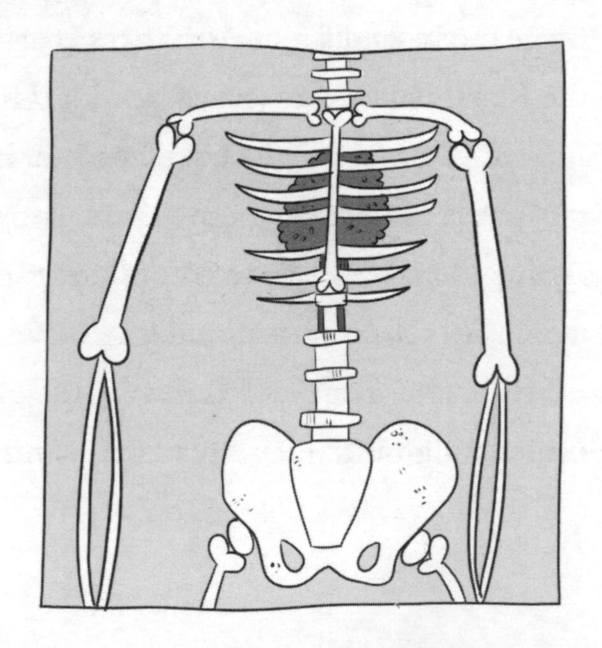

'We're flying with Kryin'Air?' grumbled Anna, looking at the departures screen. 'It's the worst airline ever! I thought Emperor Sam had super-powered rockets?'

Their plane looked less nice than a super-powered rocket, but made just as much noise (*CREEAAAK! CRAAACKK!!*). They watched it flap its wings lazily to the landing strip, ready for boarding. Like every Kryin'Air plane, the passengers had to run on treadmills to make the engines work. On this flight, they were the only passengers, but around them three thousand hamsters in little wheels helped too.

King Steve only ran half-heartedly for two minutes before declaring he was royally tired. So instead of running, he told the story of his sad childhood.

'Sam was the oldest, before me and our sister Sharon. He was better-looking, more intelligent and more fun. He was everyone's favourite – my parents', the country's, the world's. Everyone loved him! Except us. We hated him. Look, here's a picture of our family.'

'Sharon was so sad to live in Sam's shadow,' the King went on, 'that she left the palace when she was only thirteen years old, never to be seen again. And then of course the Empress of Americanada fell for Sam, and he married her and became the Emperor. So I ended up staying in Britland and being King in the Royal Palace here, where there are only five grown-up soft-play areas.'

'Oh, poor you,' Anna snorted. 'That's *such* a sad life.'

'It is!' said the King. 'Oh, look – there's a map of where we're going!'

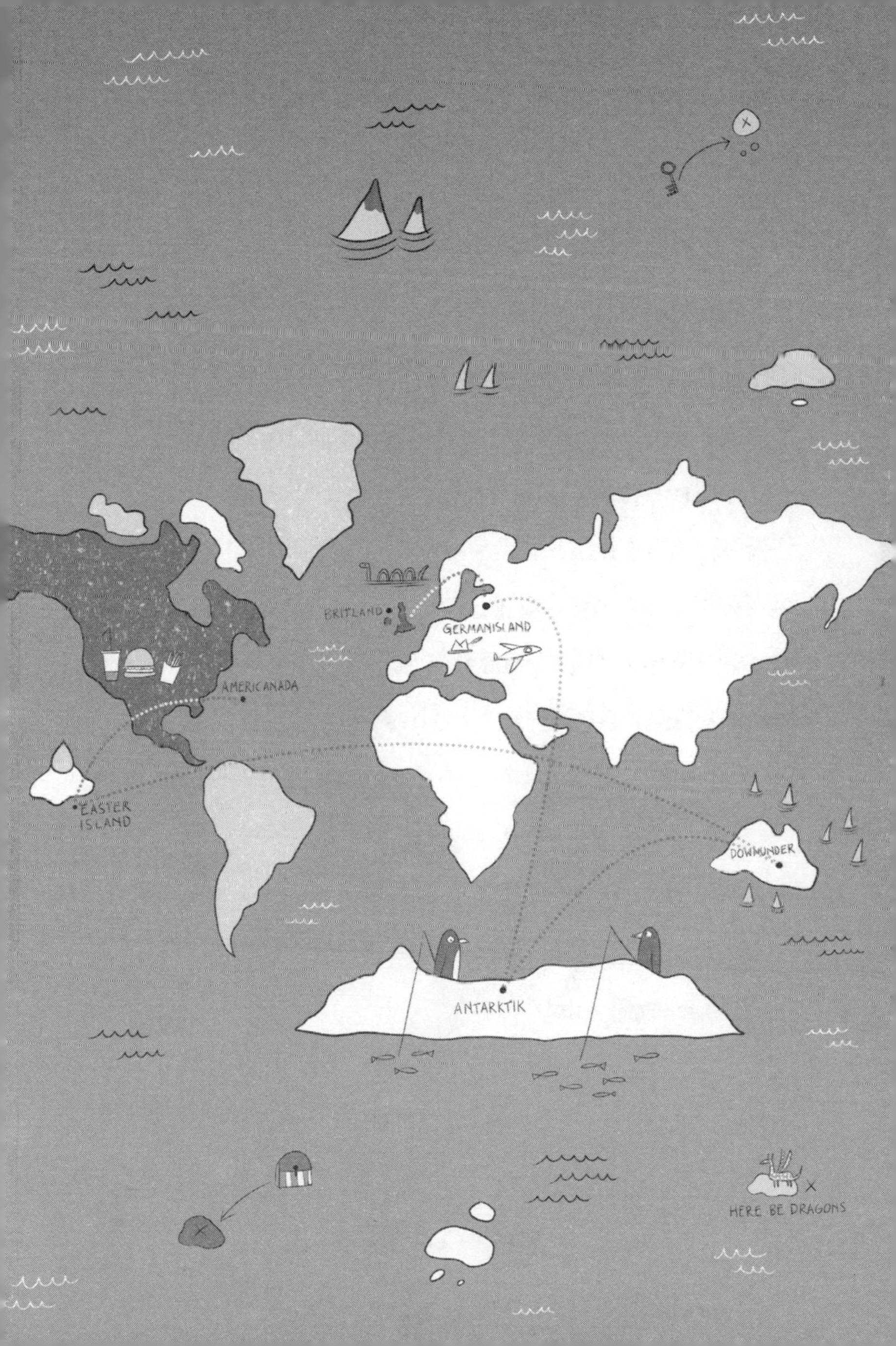

BRITLAND

GERMANISLAND

AMERICANADA

EASTER ISLAND

DOWNUNDER

ANTARKTIK

HERE BE DRAGONS

'What?!' Anna exclaimed. 'We're not going straight to Americanada?'

'Are they even going to provide in-flight entertainment?' the King asked. 'I'm getting bored. And it smells of hamster poo.'

Grumpily, he sat next to a window and spent the next half hour asking when they'd get there, singing nursery rhymes and picking at the seams of his coat. Then he fell asleep, dribbling into his beard.

'Finally, some peace and quiet,' Holly huffed. 'I know he's your dad, Pepino, but babysitting him is hard work.'

'The plane's landing,' Anna observed. 'We'll be able to stop running for a bit.'

The plane stopped at Sheriffhood Airport in Germanisland, where all the hamsters were changed for new ones and someone else got on the plane.

'Hallo,' said the newcomer. 'I belief I haf not had ze pleasure to meet you before. I am ze Über-Sheriff of Germanisland, and zis is mein assistant.'

'I see,' said Holly. 'You're one of the contestants for the Royal Bake Off?'

'Yes!' the Sheriff nodded. 'I am an expert of apfelstrudel, pretzels and prinzregententorte!'

'Well,' Anna said, 'you'd better start running, Your Über-Majesty! We're going round the world!'

'Oh, I sink I'd razzer sleep a bit while you all run,' said the Über-Sheriff, and he fell asleep next to King Steve.

'I hate royalty,' Anna groaned. 'Where to next?'

Next, they precariously skidded to a stop at the icy Emirate Airport in Antarktik. The hamsters were changed for some frozen-looking ones, who seemed grateful to be asked to run. The newcomer was the Emir of Antarktik himself, with his two helpers.

'Since you are all running so well,' said the Emir politely, 'I will read my book instead.'

He sat down next to King Steve and the Über-Sheriff, opened a book called *Baking from A to Z*, and fell asleep at the letter B.

It was a long time until the next stop, since they had to journey to the other side of the planet to the immense land of Downunder and its Imperial Airport. The new hamsters ran backwards and upside down.

The Empress of Downunder boarded the flight. She picked a treadmill and started running so vigorously that the plane was significantly faster on the next stretch of its journey.

They soon landed at Princely Airport, Easter Island.

'Is this where Easter bunnies come from?' Pepino asked excitedly.

'It might be,' said Anna. 'Look – they're bringing bunnies on instead of hamsters.'

The person who boarded was by far the

oddest royal, and her wooden assistants the most mysterious.

'Good afternoon,' said the new passenger softly. 'I am the Easter Princess.'

And she picked a treadmill and walked slowly on it, with seriousness and grace.

'Even weirder royals than ours,' said Anna. 'This Royal Bake Off is going to be very interesting …'

Chapter Three

They arrived at the capital of Americanada, Bigapple, as the night fell. The city was an amazing explosion of lights, advertising everything from sandwiches to underpants.

'Daddy,' said Pepino, shaking King Steve. 'We've arrived! You need to wake up.'

'No, Mummy, I dunwanna go to school,' grumbled the King. 'The other kids are mean to me.' He then opened an eyelid. 'Oh, phew, what a terrible dream! Where are we?'

'Just getting to Bigapple.'

'Oh, no! That's an even worse nightmare.'

On an island facing the city, the Apple of Liberty shone Granny Smith green in the dark, catching and reflecting the twinkle of the capital.

'Beautiful!' said Holly.

'Well,' King Steve snorted, 'it would be better with a climbing wall on the side and a waffle bar at the top.'

They waited for the other contestants to get off the creaky plane before they did. Then they stood outside the door and blinked.

FLASHFLASHFLASHFLASH!

‘Is it just me or have we landed in a TV studio?’ asked Anna.

Indeed the landing strip had been turned into a gigantic stage and a huge audience wheeled in and all around the Kryin’Air plane were now hovering …

‘Filmcrews!’ Pepino mused. ‘I’ve never seen real ones before.’

'And this looks like the Emperor's guest of honour, his brother Steve!' exclaimed a strong, twangy male voice through the amplifiers.

'Look at his adorable old-style Britland pants!' quavered an older female voice.

'They can see my pants?' shuddered King Steve.

'I think they mean "trousers",' explained Holly.

'And who are those *cuuute* Britlander children?' the singsong lady's voice resonated.

'How totally awesome are those crooked

yellow teeth of theirs?' boomed the man's voice. 'I hear it's a rule in Britland that teeth should never be straight or white. And we must respect that custom!'

'Enough,' Anna exclaimed. 'We're here to take part in a baking contest, not to be talked about like exotic monsters!'

'Listen to this amazing accent!' said the man's voice. 'Ex-*ott*-ic! How *exodic* is that?'

From the blinding camera flashes emerged Emperor Sam, who climbed the stairs athletically to greet them.

'Emperor Sam, nice to meet you!' he said.

'Good evening,' said Anna sternly, shaking his hand.

'You're looking a bit tired!' said the Emperor.

'You would be too if you'd been running on a treadmill all day,' retorted Anna.

'Running on a treadmill all day!' exclaimed the male voiceover. 'That's the way to go, Americanada!'

'Those Uropeans certainly know how to keep healthy,' agreed the woman.

The Emperor walked up to Holly, who turned red, held out the wrong hand and finally stammered, 'Good morning, Your Emperorship, erm, Your Imperial Highness, erm –'

'Call me Sam!' the Emperor roared. (The amplified male voice immediately commented, 'No stiff Britlander protocol for Emperor Sam!')

Then Emperor Sam planted himself in front of King Steve.

'Oh, Stevie,' said Sam, choking back tears.

'How happy I am to be with you again.'

'Well, quite,' said King Steve, and he coughed. 'Nice weather, huh?'

'Deep down in my heart, I know you must have resented me,' said Emperor Sam. 'I'm so sorry I was so much better than you at everything. This is' – he sobbed a bit – 'your opportunity to shine, Stevie.'

And he hugged his brother.

'Brotherly love!' the singsong lady's voice marvelled as the audience cheered.

'An undying bond – the truest of them all,'

commented the invisible man's voice.

Emperor Sam quickly wiped away his tears, which left his eyes absolutely not red nor swollen, and turned towards the cameras.

'Americanada! I officially declare the first Royal Bake Off open! Please welcome our hosts, Charlus Rockamel and Molly Flumpkin!'

There was a gigantic roar from the audience. The stage began to shake and a hole opened in the ground near them. Slowly, in a cloud of pink smoke, a gigantic cake emerged – and from it leapt the hosts.

'My dear little choux, let the royal baking start!' quaked Molly Flumpkin. 'In the next four days, we'll have increasingly finger-licking-licious –'

'But *devilishly difficult* baking tasks!' interrupted Charlus. 'Our contestants will have to fight against not just flour, eggs and oven times, but also fire …'

'What?' went Anna.

'… ice …'

'Pardon?' whispered Holly.

'… monsters …'

'Oh, not monsters *again*!' groaned Pepino.

'… and even more scarytastic, terrifying dangers!'

'I'll leave you in charge of those, kids,' said King Steve. 'I'll need to focus on the baking.'

'But also really nice glazed cherries,' Molly promised.

'The motto of this Royal Bake Off,' Charlus said, 'is … CAKE OR DEATH!'

'CAKE OR DEATH! CAKE OR DEATH!' the crowd chanted.

'Oh, *great*,' grumbled Anna, rolling her eyes. 'I should have guessed it wouldn't just be a matter of measuring out flour in fluid ounces.'

'I don't like this motto,' piped Molly. 'Why can't it be about cinnamon buns instead?'

'Why not cinnamon buns AND death?' Charlus yelled. 'Tomorrow, the first task will take our contestants to the scorchingly frazzling, red hot, snake-infested Grand Yeswecanyon!'

'*OOOOHHHHH!*' went the crowd, as threatening music started and a red light shone on the contestants.

'Anna, Pepino, look,' Holly muttered. 'Where are the Easter assistants going?'

The Easter Princess's assistants had jumped off the stage and were heading down the darkened landing strip.

'I don't want to stay here either! I'm leaving too,' Pepino said.

'For once, I agree with Pepino,' said Anna. 'Let's go. No one's looking at us.'

Charlus and Molly were now interviewing the contestants, and the Filmcrews were busy fluttering around them. Holly, Anna and Pepino discreetly fled the stage.

'Look,' Holly whispered. 'What are they up to?'

The three Easter Island assistants had stopped some way down the landing strip from them and were talking animatedly, staring across the Bay of Bigapple beyond the airport.

'Too far,' said one of the assistants to the others.

'Try,' said another one.

The first Easter assistant plunged its wooden hand into its wooden body and extracted what looked like …

'An Easter egg!' Pepino whispered

The egg glistened in the moonlight; it was made of metal. The Easter assistants flicked the

egg's steel ribbon to the right: a harsh red laser beam burst out at the top and a coil popped out of its side.

The trio quivered with excitement as they laid the egg down on the ground, pointing the laser beam at the Apple of Liberty.

'Go!' said one of the assistants, and the egg sprang off its coil, disappearing at high speed into the night.

‘Into the sea,’ said one of the Easter assistants. ‘Too far, as I said.’

‘We’ll find a way,’ said the second one.

‘We’ll find a way,’ repeated the third one.

And they all walked away.

‘Well, well, well,’ said Anna. ‘I don’t know what they’re here for, but clearly it’s not just to win the Royal Bake Off.’

Chapter Four

The contestants' hotel rooms were on the top floor of the hundred-storey cake skyscraper. The walls were made of tooth-breakingly hard caramel. It was impossible to have a shower, since the taps only supplied golden syrup. But the three children were too tired to notice: they all fell asleep in a pile on the bed. King Steve had slept very well on the plane, so he spent the night reading comic books and munching on his complimentary marzipan bathrobe.

The next morning, Anna, Holly, Pepino and King Steve were woken up by a flying Filmcrew crashing into their room through the windowpane, which was made of hard, transparent candy.

'Oh, boy! Take a peek at those totally kooky PJs!' roared Charlus's voice. And the presenter slipped into the room too, standing with Molly on a purple hovercraft whose spectacular flames melted the nougat carpet.

'Hey!' Anna protested. 'You can't just come into our room like this!'

'We're on a hovercraft, sweetie pie – we can do whatever we want,' said Molly. 'Big smiles for the Filmcrew!'

Anna made a face at the camera.

'She's got grit, that one!' Charlus shouted. 'Will she be the contestant everyone loves to hate? Only way to find out is to get baking! This way to the Grand Yeswecanyon!'

'This way' was a road which started right outside their window and unrolled into the distance, floating high above the earth, suspended by strong cables to the clouds above.

'Bring the Pony Cars!' Charlus shouted. A muffled noise of hooves followed and a few seconds later five Pony Cars stopped near them, whinnying welcomingly.

‘OK, this is pretty cool,’ Pepino said, and even Anna admitted it looked like fun.

The contestants stepped out of the windows on the top floor of the building and got into their cars.

‘Looks like Emperor Sam’s assistants are more prepared than us to “bake or die”,’ Anna remarked, glancing over at them. They were all wearing chefs’ hats and carrying kitchen utensils shaped like weapons.

'Ready?' Charlus shouted.

'Go!' piped Molly.

And the Pony Cars neighed into action, galloping down the floating highway.

'Your Majesty,' said Anna to King Steve as they whizzed past skyscrapers, 'can I ask you a question? The Apple of Liberty, on the island – what's in there?'

'Nothing,' said the King. 'It's made of solid bronze. It was a wedding gift from the King of Francia to Sam. Of course he always gets the best gifts. What did *I* get as a wedding present from the Francians? Just a head of garlic, not even in wrapping paper. Why do you ask?'

'Just wondering,' Anna murmured.

The Pony Cars were going so fast that the landscape under the road was just a blur: mountains, lakes, forests, deserts, more mountains. And finally, the road began to drop.

Very steeply.

Very, *very* steeply.

Towards …

'The Grand Yeswecanyon!' The two presenters' excited voices resonated above the Britlanders' heads.

'Bit hot,' King Steve noted. 'Do you think I can go topless?'

'Please don't,' Anna implored. 'You'd, erm – catch sunburn.'

'Oh, look!' said Pepino. 'So many Filmcrews are flying above our heads!'

'I think it's mostly hungry eagles, actually,' Holly pointed out.

VRROOOOOOM! The presenters' hovercraft descended into the canyon. The contestants and their assistants got out of their Pony Cars, attracting a flock of busy Filmcrews.

'Look at that sunshine!' marvelled Molly's mellow voice. 'Did you know, my lovelies, that we call this place the World's Greatest Natural Oven? Ideal for the task – you'll have to bake cupcakes in the heat of the sun –'

'But don't get *yourself* baked by it!' declared Charlus, making Molly wince. 'Only way for you to get baking is to, let's say, *convince* some creatures to lend you essential ingredients for the cupcakes … For starters, frazzling firefoxes! Find their holes and you might smuggle out some milk …'

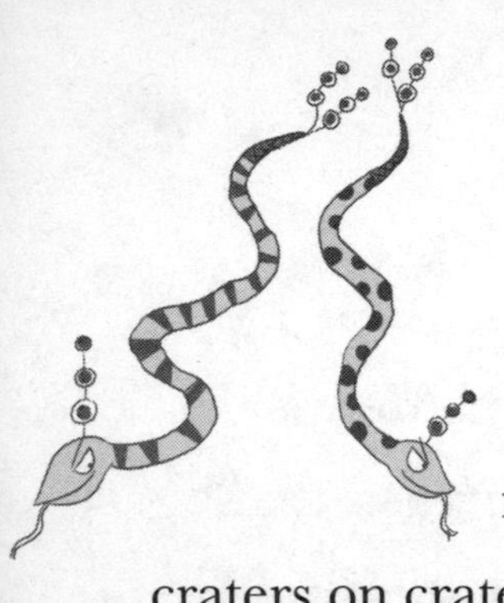

'Violently venomous rattlesnakes! Curled in their craters on crates of fresh flour ...'

'Vicious vultures! Their nests are up there – and the only path is a bit tight ... But you'll have to risk it if you want eggs!'

'And many other ingredients are here and there, under stones, among scab-inducingly scalding, scar-inducingly scorching scarabs and scorpions –'

'But all these little creatures have lovely souls really!' Molly interrupted.

'Remember,' said Charlus, 'the cupcakes have to be cooked by the time the sun disappears! Ready? Three – two – one – CAKE OR DEATH!'

'All right,' said Anna. 'Holly, you try to find those firefoxes. Pepino, you're in charge of the rattlesnakes.'

'What? But they're violently venomous!'

'Would you rather go up there and get the eggs instead?'

‘Erm, no.’

‘Then get that flour. I’ll get the eggs. Meanwhile, King Steve, if you could find the other ingred– … King Steve? Where’s he gone?’

‘Over there,’ said Holly, ‘under that tree in the shade.’

‘Tree’ was not quite the right word, nor was ‘under’, nor indeed ‘shade’.

‘What are you doing, Your Majesty?’ asked Anna. ‘You need to find ingredients for the cupcakes!’

‘That’s exactly what I’m doing,’ said the King,

and he turned over a tiny pebble next to him, and then another one, saying, 'No ingredient! No ingredient! Still no ingredient! Oh, a red ant!'

'Anna,' said Pepino, 'there's smoke coming out of your nostrils.'

'Please take her away,' said the King. 'It's hot enough without her setting herself on fire. I'll keep looking.'

Anna marched off, still fuming. Holly soon came across a firefoxes' hole. But another contestant's assistant had found it too.

'Go away,' said Holly to the polar bear. 'You're terrifying the firefoxes! They'll never leave their hole if you stay.'

'*GROAR*,' replied the Emir of Antarktik's assistant.

Holly tried to push him aside, but the bear wouldn't budge. Even worse: the other assistant came to his rescue.

'What?' Holly cried, staring in disbelief at the snowman. 'How are *you* not totally melted?'

'We trained with the Emir,' replied the snowman in a flaky voice. 'We learnt to withstand hot temperatures. I melted all the time at first, but now I'm – almost – completely – myself ...'

Almost, but not quite – for the polar bear, who was now juggling the firefox and its two babies, was showering the snowman with fireballs ...

Soon, what was left of the assistant wasn't a pretty sight.

'*Groar?*' groaned the polar bear.

'Yes, keep juggling,' said Holly, reaching into the foxes' hole. 'You're getting really good at this!'

'*GROAR!*' replied the bear, his fur beginning to turn smoke grey.

Holly dived into the hole and unhooked a jug of warm, hazelnut-smelling milk from the mantelpiece of the underground house.

She then ran away again, narrowly avoiding the firefoxes that the polar bear was throwing at her.

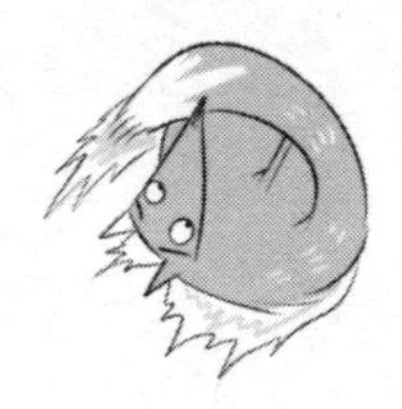

'Milk's here!' said Holly joyfully as she got back to King Steve. 'Where's Pepino?'

'Gone to get more ingredients. He found me a jar of honey and said I couldn't eat it all,' said the King, 'so I only ate half of it.'

'Well, don't eat any more,' Holly sighed, rolling her eyes. 'And don't drink any of the milk, OK?'

'OK,' said the King, but he still dipped his fingers in the jar to taste it.

'And where's Anna?'

'Up there. I've been watching her for ten minutes. It's a lot of fun. Sam's helpers collected all the ingredients in no time, but now the Empress of Downunder has sent her assistants too …'

He pointed to a tightrope high above. Anna was edging along it towards a vulture's nest in the rocky face of the canyon, with the Empress's three assistants close behind. Holly gasped.

'She'll get them easily,' the King yawned. 'They don't even have weapons.'

But the three assistants pulled something out of their pockets …

'Boomerangs!' the King exclaimed. 'That's exciting.'

'Anna!' Holly screamed. 'JUMP!'

She did – just in time.

The boomerangs whizzed towards the vulture's nest, overtook it … came back again …

And knocked three fat eggs out of the nest and on to the tightrope!

Quickly, Anna jumped again, sending the three assistants of the Empress of Downunder tumbling down …

And the eggs tumbling up … right into her arms!

'Well done!' the King clapped. 'I should hire you as my court jester.'

'Anna, are you OK?' Holly screamed.

Anna smiled at her and gave her a thumbs up – but just then the rope *snapped*.

And Anna fell!

Chapter Five

'*AAAHHHHHHHHHHH!!!!!!!!*'

'CAKE OR DEATH!' Charlus shouted from the hovercraft. 'The first victim of the Royal Bake Off!'

Three Filmcrews fluttered over, greedily catching Anna's desperate face on camera as she plunged through the air …

And she grabbed on to one of them!

CRASH! They fell on the desert floor.

'Are you all right, my darling?' Molly asked, as the presenters' hovercraft dashed towards the scene. 'Let me see those little scratches ...'

'Little scratches!' Charlus snorted. 'She's done more damage to our equipment than herself!'

Anna got up and ran over to King Steve and Holly with the eggs, which were still in one piece. 'Where's Pepino?'

'Here!' said the prince. 'I've found some flour. The problem is, I got stung by scorpions and bitten by snakes. I'm probably going to die.'

He did indeed look like the animals had taken a liking to him.

'Oh no,' said his father, 'that would be sad. But you've got six little brothers to be kings of Britland instead of you.'

'CAKE OR DEATH!' Charlus yelled, flying towards them so fast that Molly almost fell off the hovercraft. 'The little Prince of Britland has been super-stung and über-bitten! He's going to die!'

'Oh, bother,' Pepino said, and keeled over on to the sand.

'AMBULANCE!' Molly screamed.

An Ambulance arrived to look after Pepino.

'Will he be OK?' Holly asked anxiously.

'Of course,' Charlus whispered. 'We need him for the other tasks.'

'The rattlesnakes are not that venomous,' Molly muttered. 'He's probably just having little nightmares right now.'

'Grrmmmmonster!' Pepino grumbled. 'Annamonster!'

'Enough,' Anna replied. 'Let's make those cupcakes. The sun is at its peak – they'll cook perfectly. Right, Your Majesty? Your Majesty? STEVE!'

'Hmm?' said the King, who had fallen asleep a little bit.

'Make those cupcakes!'

'It's nap time!'

Anna grabbed a passing rattlesnake by the bell and dangled it above the King's head. '*Make those cupcakes*,' she growled.

'OK, OK!'

The King gathered the flour, eggs, milk, honey and other ingredients, and began to bake.

'Aaaaand they're STARTING!' yelled Charlus.

'Of course,' Molly commented, a little red, 'our dashing Emperor gathered all the ingredients in no time. Look how strongly he's mixing them together! You can see all his arm muscles bul–'

'But what's King Steve doing now?' interrupted Charlus. 'Oh, he's using red ant extract – daring choice, ladies and gentlemen, daring choice!'

'Red ant extract?' the King grumbled. 'I

thought it was strawberry syrup!'

(Anna discreetly spat out the spoonful of red liquid she'd stolen from the table.)

'He's sprinkling beetle powder on top of his icing ...'

'Am I? Looked like cocoa to me!'

'Deary me!' Molly whistled. 'Britland's got a reputation for bland food, but what explosive baking! Anaconda fangs on top of cupcakes!'

'Aren't they blanched almonds?' King Steve wondered.

'And the sun's beginning to set ...' said Charlus. 'Will the cupcakes cook before it's too late?'

‘Get them into the oven quick, Your Majesty!’ Anna cried. ‘I didn’t almost die for nothing, you know.’

King Steve opened the oven, which was made out of stones, using his own beard as oven gloves. Next to him, Emperor Sam chuckled: he’d already put his cupcakes in the oven, his hands safely tucked in fireproof, designer salamander-skin oven gloves.

'Aaaaaand Britland's cupcakes are IN THE OVEN!' Charlus yelled.

'Oh, fiddlesticks, one contestant's cupcakes aren't ready,' said Molly. 'What happened to the sweet Emir of Antarktik?'

'One of my assistants melted,' the Emir explained, shooting dark glances at Holly.

'Do you mean you have no cupcakes, Your Emirship?' Charlus asked.

'Well, they're not quite as polished as the other teams',' he replied, producing a single, sad-looking cake.

'We used my former assistant's nose,' the Emir went on, looking down at the carrot sticking out of the top, and the polar bear wiped a tear.

The cupcakes cooked in the orange setting sun. Then the teams presented the results of their baking.

'And who will have the delightful task of tasting those luscious-looking cupcakes?' Molly mused, poking Charlus in the ribs.

Charlus stared at his co-host. 'You first, Molly.'

'Oh, come on, you cheeky boy,' said Molly. 'You know you want to.'

'How fabtastic,' Charlus stammered. 'Can't absolutely not wait! Joy and deliciousness. Yummy, yummy.'

He swallowed the Americanadian cupcakes effortlessly, but only took a tiny bite of the others. 'Wanna try, Molly?'

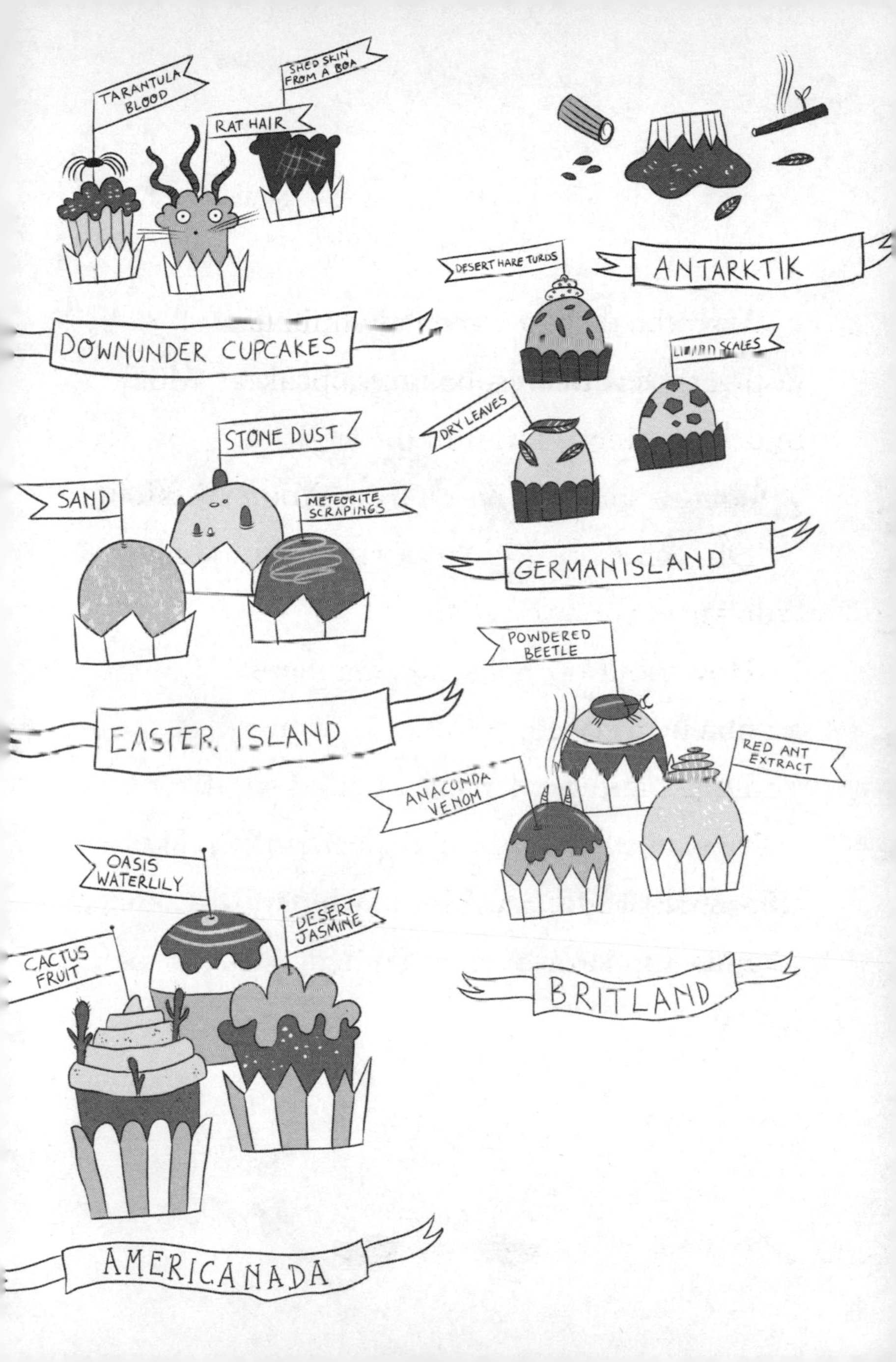

TARANTULA BLOOD
SHED SKIN FROM A BOA
RAT HAIR
DOWNUNDER CUPCAKES
STONE DUST
SAND
METEORITE SCRAPINGS
EASTER ISLAND
OASIS WATERLILY
DESERT JASMINE
CACTUS FRUIT
AMERICANADA
ANTARKTIK
DESERT HARE TURDS
SCALES
DRY LEAVES
GERMANISLAND
POWDERED BEETLE
RED ANT EXTRACT
ANACONDA VENOM
BRITLAND

'I'm on a diet,' the old lady smiled.

After a few interesting faces,

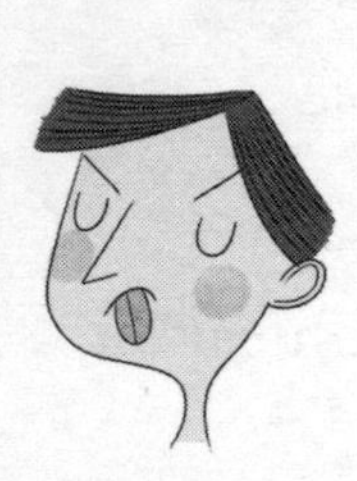  

he finally declared:

'Ladies and gentlemen, I think I speak for everyone with a crush on cupcakes when I say that EMPEROR SAM is the winner!'

'*Me?*' Emperor Sam exclaimed, trying to look

surprised. 'I don't know what to say, it's such an honour!'

He jumped on the hovercraft and kissed the hosts' cheeks, making Molly stumble dangerously.

'Unfortunately,' said Charlus, 'the contestant who's going to leave us today is …'

Silence.

Silence.

Silence.

'We'll tell you after the advert br–'

'Oh, for goodness' sake,' said Anna. 'We all

know it's the Emir of Antarktik. Everyone can see his cupcake is a complete failure.'

'How *mean*!' Molly exclaimed.

'You surprise-ruining wet Britlander blanket,' said Charlus. 'Well, all right then. The loser is the Emir of Antarktik!'

The Emir bowed and the polar bear walked with him to his Pony Car.

'How heartbreaking, saying goodbye to contestants we love so much!' said Molly tearfully.

'Can we go now?' Holly asked.

'Don't you want to be interviewed at length about how amazing it feels to be runner-up in this first task?' asked Charlus, indignant.

'Not at all,' said Anna.

'I do!' said King Steve. 'After all, it was thanks to me.'

‘We’ll leave you to it, then,’ Anna whispered. ‘Come on, Holly. Let’s get Pepino.’

In the Ambulance, Pepino opened an eyelid. ‘Am I completely dead?’

‘Not quite,’ said Anna. ‘I’m afraid they’re still expecting you to compete tomorrow.’

Chapter Six

'*W**hy did that rope snap?*'

It was eleven o'clock at night. King Steve had been asleep for hours, but Anna was keeping Holly and Pepino awake.

'Come on, Anna,' said Holly. 'It could have been anything. A falling rock, a loose knot –'

'Or maybe you were a bit too heavy,' said Pepino. 'I don't mean to be rude, but with all those croissants you ate in Parii …'

'No,' said Anna. 'When I was standing on the rope, I clearly felt someone was … hacking at it. There were three tugs. It went *hack, hack, hack.*'

Knock, knock, knock.

The three children jumped. The sound had come from the window, whose candy-panes had been freshly replaced.

'Who's there?' asked Holly.

They heard a whisper:

'The Emir. Please open the window. I'm in a not-very-comfortable position.'

They opened the window and rescued the not-very-comfortably-positioned Emir.

'Have you come to tell me off about your assistant?' asked Holly as they dragged him into the bedroom. 'I'm sorry he melted. But he wasn't the best person to take to a hot country.'

'No,' the Emir said. 'I have come to warn you …' He turned to Anna. 'The Über-Sheriff of Germanisland tried to *kill* you today.'

Anna gasped.

'My assistant saw him hacking at the rope you were standing on – with an axe.'

'I knew it!' Anna exclaimed.

'I heard him say to his assistants, "That dirty little Miss Know-It-All has got what she deserves!" And then he laughed like this: "Mwahahahahaha!"'

'I've told you this before, Anna,' said Pepino. 'You rub people up the wrong way. They see you, and then they want you to fall to your death.'

'Hey!' Anna retorted. 'Don't make it sound like it's *my* fault! Thanks for telling us, Your Emirship. Sounds like we'd better visit our Germanislander neighbours … Come on, team!'

'What, *now*?' Pepino moaned. 'I thought we were watching TV tonight.'

'Doesn't look like there's anything interesting on,' Holly said, flipping through the channel guide.

'Let's go,' said Anna. 'Which room is the Germanislander team in?'

'Room five. But you can't go through the

door,' said the Emir. 'There are Fans camping in the corridor. They'll ask you for autographs, and then they'll eat you up, they love you so. That's why I had to crawl outside the window.'

Anna looked through the peephole at the crowded hallway. 'Brrrr. They look scary. We'll go over the roof.'

'What?' Pepino moaned. 'I'd much rather watch all those adverts!'

'Hurry up, Pepino. We haven't got all night!'

Anna opened the window and stood on the slim ledge, feeling for the roof above. Holly gave her a leg-up, and she heaved herself on to the roof. She then pulled Holly and Pepino up.

'This way!' Anna called.

They ran across the flat roof of the skyscraper.

'We won't be able to stand on that window ledge,' said Holly as they knelt down near the edge and peered over. 'Two of us will have to hold the third one by his feet, head down.'

'What do you mean, "by *his* feet?"' Pepino asked. 'What if we decide to pick a *girl* for this?'

'Don't be silly, Pepino,' said Anna. 'Her skirt would turn over and you'd see her pants.'

'But *you're* not wearing a skirt,' he observed.

'*ARGHHHH!!!*'

The two girls had grabbed his legs.

'*Shh!*' whispered Anna. 'Listen carefully to what they say.'

And they tipped Pepino over the edge. He was so surprised he didn't even manage to scream; instead, he held on to his crown and swung towards the window.

While Pepino was listening, Holly nudged her sister. 'Why do you think the Über-Sheriff would target *you*? Why would he care?'

'Maybe he's hired by Emperor Sam to kill everyone else's assistants,' Anna whispered.

'I don't believe it. Emperor Sam is arrogant, but he's not a killer.'

'How can you tell? Oh, hang on. Pepino's kicking,' Anna murmured. 'Let's pull him up.'

'So?' they said, after hauling him up and back on to his feet.

'My head is full of all the blood in my body!'

Pepino groaned. 'My ears are going *POMPOM! POMPOM!* I think my heart's fallen into my skull.'

Anna tapped him on the head to help his heart fall back into place. 'Well? What did they say?'

'The Über-Sheriff said he'd missed us this time, but not tomorrow – "Tomorrow there will be deaths, the deaths of those Britlander kids!" That's what he said. And his assistant kept saying, "You'll be marvellous," and calling him all kinds of little nicknames.'

'Great,' Anna winced. 'So he *does* want to kill us. Anything else?'

'Well,' said Pepino, 'he had a different voice.'

'Different how?'

'Completely different. He didn't haf zat fery schtrong Germanislander accent any more.'

Chapter Seven

That night, Holly, Anna, Pepino and King Steve dreamt that they were being carried around by a helicopter. And when the morning came, they were woken up by the sound of running water.

'Didjuleavthetapon, Pepino?' King Steve mumbled.

'That'd be a *very* big tap,' Anna commented, sitting up on her bed.

They weren't in their hotel room any more. They weren't even in Bigapple. The sound of running water – or, rather, of crashing, thrashing, smashing water – was coming from …

A HUGE waterfall.

'Aaaaand the Britlander contestants are *finally* waking up!' Charlus yelled. 'Hurry up, the second task starts in three minutes.'

'Where *are* we?' Anna asked, stepping out of bed on to the island and looking around.

'I recognise this place,' said Holly. 'The N.H.E.A.G.A.R.A. Falls. The biggest, most dangerous waterfall in the world.'

'N.H.E.A.G.A.R.A?' Anna repeated.

'It stands for "Nobody Has Ever A'crossed the Gigantic Awful River Alive", sweetie,' replied Molly.

All the royal contestants, still in their pyjamas (apart from Emperor Sam, who was wearing a light blue suit, with his helpers in military gear) lined up on the small island while the beds were being carried away by small helicopters.

'Today you won't need any baking powder, but you'll need some baking *power*! Your mission is to bake a floating island. Easy enough, right?' Charlus grinned.

'Whisked egg whites and sugar dropped into a nice little pool of custard,' Molly whispered.

Charlus added, 'All the ingredients for the custard are on this island. But the eggs must be taken from a nest of crocodiles, and the only way to whisk the whites is to put them in a barrel and run on it at top speed on the edge of the falls! Ready? CAKE OR DEATH!'

The two hosts floated off. Emperor Sam, whistling the Americanadian anthem, started making custard, while his assistants jumped into the water to collect ingredients. The Über-Sheriff, Anna noted, was whispering things into his assistant's ear, and both were looking intently at the Britlander team. The Empress of Downunder, meanwhile, dived into the river, followed by her three assistants.

'OK, children,' said King Steve. 'Today I promise I'll be good. I'll help you more than yesterday.'

'Great,' said Holly. 'You're getting the crocodile eggs, then?'

'Uh, no. I'll find the ingredients for the custard instead.'

'Look, they're right here on the table behind you!'

'Oh! Found them!' King Steve exclaimed. 'Brilliant. I'll make the custard.'

'Right,' said Anna. 'Can anyone here swim well? Pepino?'

'Only with floats,' confessed the prince.

'Oh, dear. Let's think of a way to –'

But she stopped mid sentence, having spotted a new visitor on the island …

A hungry-looking crocodile came crawling towards them. It tried to eat Anna.

Then Holly.

Then Pepino.

'Hey! My crown!' Pepino yelled, as the crocodile slithered back into the water with it.

'Leave it, Pepino!' said Holly. 'Who cares? At least it wasn't your face.'

'I'd rather it were!' Pepino grouched. 'I got *so* told off by Mum and Dad for losing my crown in Parii. This is a brand new one and it tells me jokes when I'm bored! That crocodile isn't taking it!'

And he *jumped* into the water.

'I thought he couldn't swim without floats,' said Holly nervously.

Indeed, Pepino immediately sank.

'CAKE OR DEATH!!!' Charlus shouted, making Molly jump so high that he had to catch her in his arms. 'The heir of Britland drowns for his crown!'

'Fantastic,' Anna grumbled. 'Come on, Holly, let's rescue him.'

They both jumped into the river and held their breath to look for Pepino. Underwater, strong currents were pulling everything towards the waterfall.

'Pepino!' Holly shouted, but it sounded like *'BBLLEPPLLIBBLLNO!'*

They grabbed on to Pepino's hand, and swam off against the current, following the crocodile.

'*Pssffhha!*' coughed Pepino as they resurfaced. 'It's very windy down there. I mean, current-y. Where's that criminal crocodile?'

'Right-t-there,' stuttered Holly, as the crocodile glided towards them, smiling, the crown on his head.

'I can't believe this!' Pepino shouted. 'He's *crowned* himself! Give – it – back!'

He ripped the crown off the crocodile's head and knocked him on the nose with it.

This did not please the crocodile *one little bit.*

He began to thrash and flap and buck – until the water was like whipped cream!

And they were all thrown up into the air and landed on a little island, near a nest.

'Careful! Don't break them!' Holly advised Pepino, who tried to grab an egg from it.

The Empress of Downunder and her assistants, not even slightly out of breath, had just got to the little island too.

'How did you swim here so fast?' the Empress asked. '*We're* used to crocodile-infested waters, but you? Anyway, boys – get those eggs.'

'Our crocodile friend isn't too happy to see his eggs taken away …' Charlus chanted, hovering their way.

'*Put me down!*' grumbled Molly, who was still in Charles's arms. 'The Filmcrews will see my knickers!'

On the island, the crocodile turned around. In one swift move, the Empress of Downunder jumped on his back and slammed his jaw shut.

'That's how you show them who's boss!' the old Empress shouted.

'There's another one over there,' Anna pointed out.

An assistant went to lock down the second crocodile in the same way.

'And another one there,' Holly politely remarked.

Another assistant leapt on the third crocodile.

'There's also a little one there,' said Pepino.

The third assistant took care of the fourth crocodile. And now they were a little stuck.

'GET THE EGGS!' Anna shouted.

'We'll never be able to swim back with them in our hands,' said Holly. 'We need a container, a basket, a … a …'

The two sisters looked at Pepino's head.

'What?' said Pepino suspiciously.

In one swift move, Holly stole his crown.

'Holly! You scheming thief! I'll have you put in jail for high treason!'

The two girls filled the crown with eggs and dived into the river again. Pepino immediately jumped after them.

'Oh, it's much easier in this direction,' Pepino remarked. 'We barely need to swim!'

'That's because of the mahoosive waterfall, remember?' spluttered Holly.

'Oh, yes,' Pepino recalled. 'We might break the eggs if we fall down there.'

'We won't fall down there,' huffed Anna. 'Grab on to that branch!'

As they passed under an overhanging tree, they reached up for a low branch and pulled themselves out of the water and on to the main island, where King Steve was joyfully ladling custard into his mouth to make sure it tasted fine.

'Oooh, here you are,' said the King. 'I can't believe you went egg picking on your own! Children grow up so fast.'

And he gave them a ginormous hug.

'I just need those whisked now, please,' said King Steve.

Anna, Holly and Pepino broke the eggs, carefully separated the yolks from the whites, and poured the whites into the wooden barrel. Then, after some effort, they forced the lid shut.

'And now what?' asked Pepino, putting his crown back on.

'Now,' said Holly, taking a deep breath, 'I'll run on top of the barrel at the edge of the waterfall. That's what the hosts said we had to do.'

'Oh, Holly!' Anna moaned. 'It's dangerous!'

'I know. But I'm the eldest, and you've already done many dangerous things.'

Anna squeezed her sister tightly. She hadn't forgotten how scared she'd been that time, not so very long ago, when Holly had been turned into a statue.

'Good luck, Holly,' said Pepino. 'If you succeed, I *won't* have you jailed for high treason.'

So they pushed the barrel into the water, and Holly climbed up and precariously walked on top of it until it reached the edge of the falls …

And then she began to RUN!

'Look at that Britlander girl!' Charlus exclaimed. 'She'd run a marathon in a few minutes!'

'I had some practice,' said Holly between clenched teeth, 'on that Kryin'Air flight …'

One of Emperor Sam's assistants, as well as the Über-Sheriff's assistant, was also preparing to run at the top of the falls.

'Oooh, what perfectly whisked egg whites!' Molly screamed. 'So snowy they're overflowing!'

Indeed, the lid of Holly's barrel appeared to have popped open – and solidly whisked egg white was bubbling out.

Holly looked down to see what was going on.

And was thrown off balance as the barrel began to tilt upright …

Until she toppled head first …

Into the egg whites!

'CAKE OR DEATH!' Charlus shouted, excitedly jumping up and down.

'Will you STOP SHAKING THIS HOVERCRAFT!' Molly shrieked.

'HOLLY!' screamed Anna and Pepino. 'Charlus, Molly! Do something!'

But it was too late!

As the barrel crashed down into the falls, Holly righted herself, grabbed the lid, pulled it down hard … and everything went dark.

When Holly woke up, she was in bed in their room in Bigapple.

'I'm fed up with being the one who always passes out,' she mumbled.

'Holly!' Anna and Pepino shouted, and went to hug her.

'I'm so glad you're awake,' said Pepino. 'Every time you're

knocked out, I have to talk to Anna and it gets tiring.'

'I know what you mean,' said Holly.

'If you're nasty to me, I won't give you any floating island,' said Anna.

But she still gave her a beautiful cup of custard with an iceberg of egg white on top, just frothy enough and just creamy enough.

'Yum! It's like eating a vanilla cloud.'

'You're officially the first person to have survived falling into the N.H.E.A.G.A.R.A. Falls,' said Pepino. 'They're going to have to

change the name to N.H.E.A.G.A.R.A.A.F.H:
"Nobody Has Ever A'crossed the Gigantic Awful River Alive Apart From Holly".'

'Emperor Sam won the task again,' said Anna, 'and the Empress of Downunder got eliminated – she didn't have enough crocodile eggs.'

'And now what?' Holly asked.

'Now we sleep until tomorrow's task,' said Pepino.

But barely had they put their heads on their pillows than there was a knock.

On the *ceiling*.

Chapter Eight

'I had to crawl into the air conditioning system so as to avoid the Fans,' explained the Empress of Downunder.

'Don't worry,' she went on, 'I'm used to hanging upside down. Listen, kids – it's about the Über-Sheriff. He wants to kill you. I saw him sawing at the hinges of your barrel lid while you were getting the eggs. It must be why the lid popped open again and you fell in,' she said, looking at Holly.

'Why would he want to kill *Holly* and not Anna?' Pepino asked.

'Hey!' Anna exclaimed.

'Thank you for telling us,' said Holly. 'Especially as we weren't very nice to you, leaving you with the crocodiles.'

'Oh,' said the Empress, 'we became quite good friends. We're taking them back to Downunder.'

She said good bye, and so did her crocodile friend who had appeared next to her.

'Right,' Anna said. 'The Über-Sheriff of Germanisland wants to kill us. I bet he's going to try again tomorrow – and we must make sure that this time, he doesn't get away with it.'

'I'll tail him,' said Pepino. 'You girls can look for the dangerous things. I mean, the ingredients.

And I will laze around behind the Über-Sheriff. I mean, do some high-danger tailing.'

Anna looked at Pepino suspiciously. 'Come on, Anna,' said Holly. 'Let Pepino do it. After all, he's very good at lazing around.'

'OK,' said Anna. 'But don't let them get away, Pepino, all right? We must make sure that –'

BANG! BANG! BANG!

More noises from the ceiling.

'Is that you, Empress?' Holly called.

'Or crocodile?' Pepino added.

No reply. Anna pushed the grid that covered

the air vent and looked inside.

'It's the Easter Princess,' she murmured, 'and her three assistants.'

'What are they doing in the ceiling at this time of the night?' Holly asked.

'I don't know. Let's follow them.'

'Oh no,' sighed Pepino, but the girls had already dragged him into the ventilation shaft.

They followed the Easter Princess and her assistants, crawling down the narrow passage. Suddenly the Princess and her assistants disappeared, and it wasn't long before Holly,

Anna and Pepino understood why … as the floor suddenly dropped away, sending them whooshing down a long, swirling slide.

'That was fun!' Pepino whispered, picking himself up at the bottom. 'Where are we?'

They had slid all the way down the skyscraper and landed near the entrance. All around them, Bigapplers were cruising down fast conveyor belts. The street beyond was full of whinnying Pony Cars, including bright yellow ones with 'TAXI' signs on their heads.

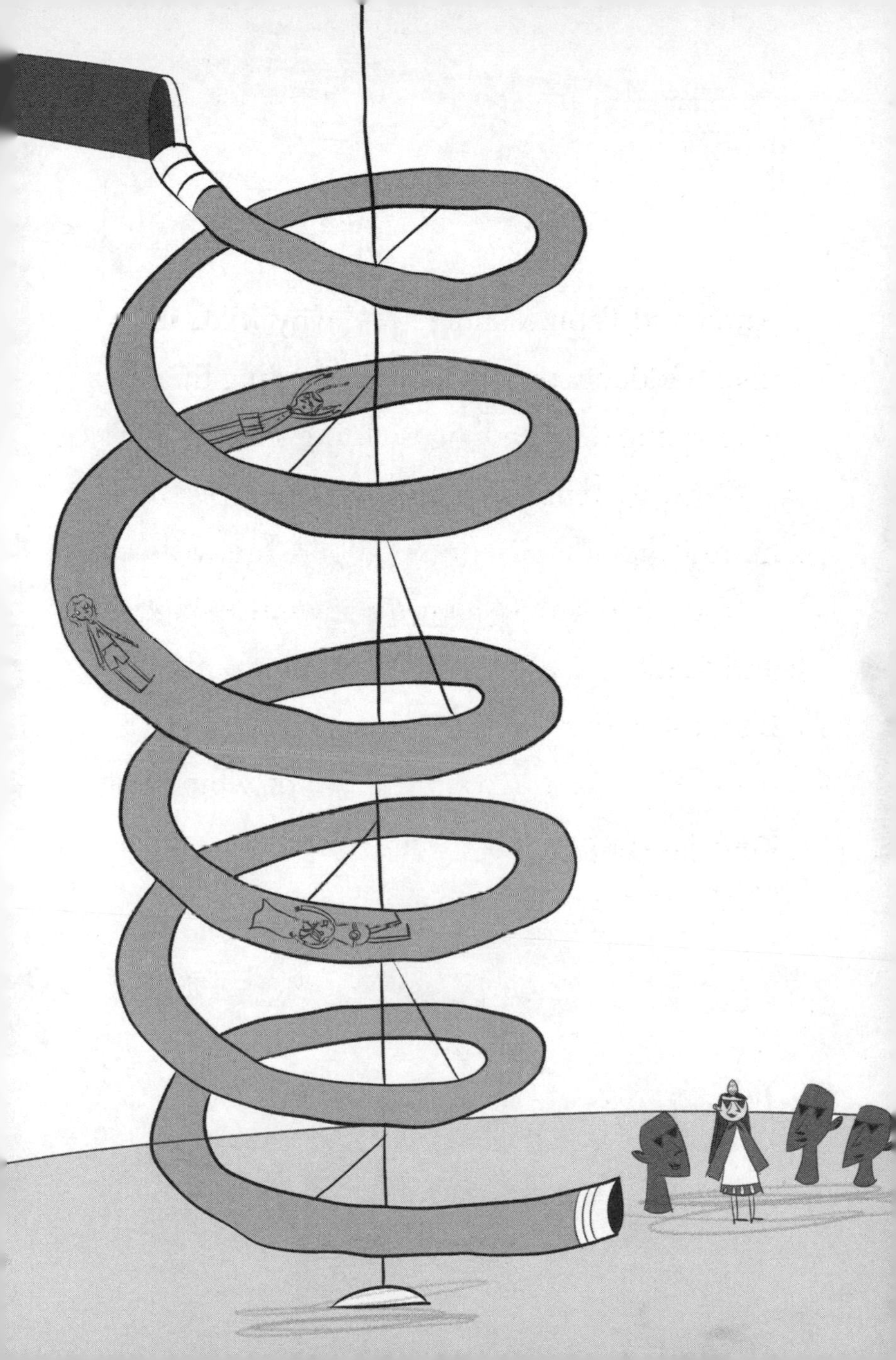

M

'Should we follow her?' Holly murmured, watching the Easter Princess and her assistants step on to one of the conveyor belts. 'What if it's a trap and she wants to kill us?'

'Not everyone wants to kill us,' replied Anna. 'Only one royal in five.'

So they jumped on to the conveyor belt and stayed on until the Princess got off a couple of blocks away, near the harbour.

There, by the bay, they were as close as they'd ever been to the Apple of Liberty, round and shiny on its little island. Anna, Holly and Pepino hung back and waited to see what the Easter Islanders would do next.

'Too far again,' said one of the wooden figures.

'Try,' said the Easter Princess.

The assistants got out the metal Easter egg and set it up on the pier as they had before. The red laser dot appeared bang in the middle of the Apple. A few seconds later, *PSHAK!* The egg sprung off and …

PLINK! The tiniest noise, in the distance, of metal against metal.

'We did it,' said one of the assistants. 'It's in there.'

'Very good,' said the Princess. 'It will take a

night and a day and a night to hatch.'

'A night and a day and a night,' they all repeated seriously.

'The day after tomorrow,' the Princess whispered, 'we will come back.'

The assistants nodded, and the strange team glided off.

'Well,' Anna said, 'I'm *really* starting to doubt that this bunch came here just for the Royal Bake Off.'

Chapter Nine

'Now, this is *cool*,' said Anna.

'Very, *very* cool,' said Pepino.

'We're going to have to go into *that?*' Holly was worried.

'That' was a ...

SUPER-POWERED ROCKET

'Royal contestants!' Charlus exclaimed, hovering above the four teams. 'You have all shown that you can bake amazingly – even in the most bizarre situations. But you haven't yet shown that you can bake in the most bizarre *positions*. And where better to do that than in a kitchen with *zero gravity*?'

'Oh, hurrah!' Pepino marvelled. 'I've always wanted to be an astronaut!'

A door on the side of the rocket opened, and a long ladder unfolded. One by one, the royal contestants and their assistants climbed up.

The inside of the rocket had four fully equipped kitchen tops and ovens attached to the curving walls.

'Fasten your seat belts for take-off! In space, even the *fattest* of you will float around like a little linnet!' Molly piped, looking pointedly at King Steve. 'Grab on tight to those spatulas and whisks! You'll have to bake … a solar system!'

'A solar system?' Anna repeated. 'How?'

'However you like! A miniature solar system, with planets and satellites made of any type of

cake. The most gorgeous and the tastiest will win!'

'And anyone who accidentally bakes a black hole will be sucked into it!' Charlus roared. 'Ready? Three! Two! One! BAKE OFF TAKE-OFF!'

The rocket made the most deafening noise as it wrenched itself from the ground.

As soon as they reached outer space, the belts unfastened, and they were all

floating

around

the

rocket

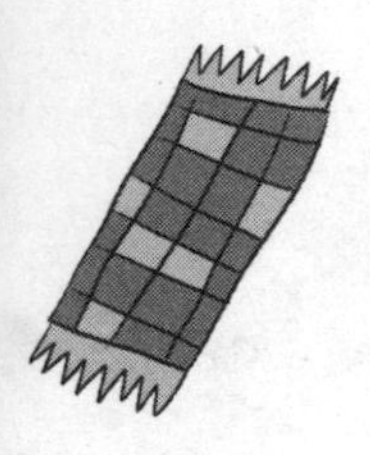

and so were

the baking

utensils!

'Keep an eye on the Easter Princess,' said Anna to Holly. 'And you, Pepino, make sure the Über-Sheriff doesn't kill us. I'll go help the King.'

'I don't need help!' King Steve mumbled. 'I'm checking that the food is good quality!'

'No, Your Majesty, you're just flying around gobbling up chocolate chips,' said Anna. 'Let's work on that solar system.'

Behind them, Sam's assistants were already drawing elaborate maps on paper while the Emperor himself combed his hair, looking at his reflection in a Filmcrew. Holly pretended to catch

some flying pralines, but she was keeping a close eye on the Easter Princess, who didn't seem too concerned with making her own solar system.

Pepino, meanwhile, was fluttering about like a sparrow near the Über-Sheriff and his assistant. His assistant was pirouetting in the air. 'I feel like I'm eighty again!'

'You mean eighteen,' said Pepino.

'No, no, eighty,' said the assistant. 'I was young and sprightly at that age.'

'Why,' said Pepino, 'how old can you possibly be now?'

The Über-Sheriff coughed. 'Solar system!' he roared. 'No time for chit-chat.'

'Of course, sweet *wienerbrød*,' said the assistant.

And they shooed Pepino away.

'How's it going, Peps?' asked Anna, who was putting into orbit a flurry of hundreds and thousands around a big caramel and chocolate planet. 'Have they tried to kill us yet?'

'No. They're too busy making their solar system. It's weird, though, Anna – they lose their Germanislander accent when they focus on work. It reminds me a bit of –'

They were interrupted by Charlus bouncing off from one wall of the rocket to their side. 'Royals might not be rocket scientists, but they're ace at cakes in space! Look at Emperor Sam's moon! Don't you just want to take a bite of it right now?'

'Chocolate and white truffle rolled in saffron and icing sugar,' yawned the Emperor. 'Easy little recipe I learnt during my Intensive Cocoa Course in Belgick.' And he flicked the moon into orbit around the Earth he'd already made, with blueberry jelly for the oceans and perfectly chiselled mint fondant for the continents.

‘And what’s the Easter Princess doing?’ Charlus asked. ‘Her assistants have made a … erm … I guess this sort of qualifies as a solar system … after an alien monster invasion!’

The Easter team’s solar system was indeed rather pitiful-looking: crumbs of mashed-up cookies and broken chocolate chips flying around an overcooked mince pie.

‘The task is almost over, royal contestants, and we’ll be judging it here and –’

BOOM!

The rocket shook.

'What was that?' asked Anna.

Anna, Pepino and Holly turned around and saw on the wall of the rocket, almost right behind them, three charred dents.

'Oh, silly Über-Sheriff of Germanisland!' Molly giggled. 'He's had a little accident!'

'I am so sorry,' said the Über-Sheriff sourly. 'I set fire to some raisins to try to make them into comets.'

'And shot them at *us*?' Anna growled. 'That's enough! Charlus, Molly, this man has tried to get us in every single task!'

Mayhem ensued.

The Über-Sheriff of Germanisland, losing

all composure, fired another salvo of burning raisins at Holly, Anna and Pepino, which they barely dodged.

'Now look here,' said King Steve, 'this isn't very fair play.'

'Throw them your sun, Dad!' Pepino screamed.

Steve hurled his orange sun at the Über-Sheriff, who retaliated with a shower of praline meteorites.

PP
A

'Take that, Britland!' the Über-Sheriff shouted, throwing them his Venus, which he'd made out of a jawbreaker.

'CAKE OR –' Charlus began to shout, but Molly stuffed his mouth with the Easter Princess's mince pie.

'Take Uranus!' Anna shouted back, hurling their giant round chiffon cake at the Über-Sheriff.

Uranus was big enough to knock the Über-Sheriff's hat off, and it hung pitifully around his neck, tied with an elastic band.

'Mummy!' the Über-Sheriff moaned. 'They knocked my hat off!'

'Wait a minute,' said Holly. 'How come you haven't had your Germanislander accent during the fight?'

'That's what I've been telling you,' said Pepino.

'Wait another minute!' Anna yelled. 'I recognise this balding scalp!'

'Balding is a strong word,' the Über-Sheriff said. 'I lose a hair or two once in a while ...'

'ALASPOORYORICK!' Anna screamed.

'This is King Alaspooryorick of Daneland, not the Über-Sheriff of Germanisland. He's the bloodthirsty killer who tried to invade Britland last week!'

'Oh, that is too unfair!' screamed the fake Über-Sheriff. 'My costume was so good!'

'And you'd worked hard on that accent,' said his assistant, taking off her hat, wig and cape.

It was Alaspooryorick's mum in an old-fashioned lacy dress.

'Incwadible!' Charlus yelled, munching through the mince pie. 'The woyal conteshtant was an IMPOSHTOR, only here to kill the Bwitland team!'

'Only the children,' Alaspooryorick rectified. 'They wrapped me in a snotty handkerchief!'

'Emperor Sam,' Anna implored, 'do something!'

Emperor Sam had been paying very little attention to the fight, so busy had he been making sure that his aniseed and gooseberry Pluto was put into orbit at just the right speed. He said lazily, 'Assistants – catch Alaspooryorick.'

'Yes, Emperor!' his assistants roared, and

they immediately fired some quickly solidifying caramel at Alaspooryorick and his mum.

‘The criminals are cloaked in caramel like caterpillars in a cocoon!’ Charlus declared. ‘Another military victory for Americanada!’

‘And more importantly,’ Molly marvelled, ‘our Imperial baker has made the most scrumptious solar system in the solar system!’

‘We’d need to taste it to make sure of that,’ Pepino stated.

And without waiting for anyone to ask, Pepino, Holly, Anna, King Steve and Molly flapped their arms and their legs to be the first to munch on the quadruple-crusted Earth (pistachio, white chocolate, nougatine and almond butter, with a marble of orange fudge in the middle), on the tiny sea salt and caramel meteorites, and on the gigantic strawberry jelly sun, warmed to just the right temperature.

Molly wiped her mouth after hoovering up the hazelnut-spread rings of Saturn. 'I declare Emperor Sam the winner!'

The Filmcrew on board clapped loudly, and Emperor Sam said, 'Oh please, don't, it's embarrassing,' twirling around like a ballerina.

'The not-Über-Sheriff-after-all is to be disqualified for cheating and trying to kill other contestants!' Charlus yelled.

'And, above all, for using *raisins* instead of chocolate chips for his cookie-flying-saucers,' added Molly. ' No one prefers raisins to chocolate chips in cookies. Say you're sorry!'

Alaspooryorick apologised, looking straight at a floating Filmcrew with a sheepish expression on his face, as the rocket made its way back to Earth:

'I'm sorry, Americanada, that I tried to kill the pesky Britlander kids. And I'm sorry that I used raisins for my cookies. I should never, ever, *ever* have used raisins.'

Chapter Ten

The final task was taking place in the giant studio in Bigapple itself – but the next day, the Easter Princess didn't turn up.

'Well, well, well!' Charlus said, tapping his watch. 'Looks like our Princess got cold feet! Maybe she was afraid of competing against the two brothers!'

'Or maybe,' mumbled Holly to Anna and Pepino, 'she's busy doing *something else*.'

Charlus and Molly waited for a flock of Filmcrews to gather around the two royal contestants and their assistants.

'Regardless,' said Molly, 'the final will take place! And no help today from your young assistants. Today, only the royal contestants will be baking.'

'Oh, shucks,' said King Steve. 'Does that mean *I* have to look for ingredients in monsters' lairs?'

'It would give us a break,' Anna sighed.

'No monsters today!' Charlus yelled. 'All the ingredients are here for you on this table.'

'It looks like a perfectly ordinary pile of ingredients,' remarked Anna.

'Your mission today,' Molly said to the two brothers, 'is to cook Americanada's national dish: an *apple pie*!'

There was an incredulous silence.

'An apple pie?' Anna repeated. '*That's* the final?'

'Yup,' said Charlus.

'After fighting crocodiles and being stung by scorpions?'

'Yes,' replied Molly.

'After being asked to bake in space?'

'Yep!' Charlus chanted. 'If anything, it's even more difficult than all that. It's *so simple* that it's difficult.'

King Steve scratched his chin. Sam had already picked up the apple peeler, and was sharpening it on a big diamond that adorned his crown.

'That's great, Daddy,' said Prince Pepino. 'You'll bake the best-ever apple pie. Remember that crab-apple crumble competition!'

'You have three hours,' said Molly. 'And

you will be judged by the strictest judges in the country – volunteers from each of our beautiful states!'

'Ready?' shouted Charlus. 'CAKE OR DEATH!'

'Death?' Holly repeated. 'What can possibly cause anyone's death in *this* task?'

'Well, not much,' Charlus confessed, 'but it's a nice jingle.'

'Let's get out of here,' Anna told Holly and Pepino. 'We *have* to find out what the Easter Princess and her assistants are up to.'

The three children ran out of the studio. In the streets of the city, excitement was mounting. Giant screens were broadcasting the final, and

Americanadians were holding flags and pictures of Emperor Sam. A couple of Britlander tourists were cheering for King Steve.

Holly, Anna and Pepino jumped on a conveyor belt that took them to the harbour.

It looked like nothing had happened to the Apple of Liberty. It was wrapped in layers of silvery fog, rising from the dark blue sea which circled the island.

Anna found a dime on the ground and dropped it into a small pair of binoculars nailed to a post in the harbour.

THE BEST EMPEROR IN THE WORLD
SAM,
SAM!
SAM, SAM,
SAM!
A GOOD
ENOUGH KING

Then she oriented the binoculars towards the Apple of Liberty. And what she saw made her spine cold and tingly.

In the side of the magnificent apple was a large hole. Anna looked around for the Princess and caught sight of a boat heading swiftly towards the island.

'The Princess is just getting to the island,' Anna declared. 'Quick – a boat! We need to stop her!'

'We *what*?' Holly jumped. 'No, we need to call the Emperor!'

'The Emperor is much too busy baking his apple pie. And the rest of the country is too busy watching him! Let's go!'

Anna jumped into a small motor boat which was moored to the pier, but its energy-drink tank was empty. But suddenly they spotted in the water …

'There! A flock of turtles!' Holly shouted.

They each picked a turtle, leapt on and were gone.

Chapter Eleven

As they drew nearer to the gigantic apple, they heard a sinister sound.

GRRRRRRRRR! GRRRRRRRRRRRR!

'Whatever hatched from that egg is *digging* into the Apple,' said Anna.

'I thought Dad said it was solid bronze?'

'That thing must be strong enough to drill through bronze …'

And suddenly *that thing* surfaced through the hole.

'Look! It's some sort of worm! It must have been in the egg,' exclaimed Anna, 'and hatched when the egg was shot into the Apple …'

'But *why is it drilling in there*?' Holly asked.

Holly turned towards the city. On a giant screen, she could just make out Emperor Sam's dashing smile; he was cutting apples into quarters for the pie.

'They're not going to finish any time soon. Where's the army?'

'Usually with my aunt, the Empress,' said Pepino, 'on top-secret military missions. Shall I phone her?'

Pepino squeezed out a phone from his pocket.

'Wow,' said Holly, 'it's not exactly the latest model.'

'My parents are cheapskates,' Pepino said sadly. He dialled his aunt's number.

'Auntie?' said Pepino. 'It's Pepino. How's everything?'

'Pepino!' the Empress exclaimed. 'How lovely of you to call your old aunt! I'm just out waging war in the Underwater

Rift of Midatlantis
in order to spread
peace and freedom.'

'That's great,' said
Pepino, 'but you might want
to come home pretty quickly.
Someone is drilling into the Apple of
Liberty.'

There was an ominous silence on the line.

'Auntie? Still here? It might be nothing, but –'

'RED, BLUE AND WHITE STAR-

SPANGLED ALERT LAUNCHED! FIGHT TO THE DEATH, PEPINO! I'LL BE THERE AS SOON AS I CAN!'

And she hung up.

'What's a red, blue and white star-spangled alert?' Pepino asked.

'I don't know,' said Holly, 'but the Princess's spotted us …'

Hopping up and down on the boat, the Easter assistants were pointing at the three children. The Princess frowned and talked quickly to the giant metallic worm, hovering above their heads, who dived back into the Apple of Liberty.

'We can't run away,' said Holly. 'We have to attack them.'

'Turtles!' Anna shouted. 'To the Princess's boat!'

The sea turtles swerved towards the boat.

'What are you doing here?' the Princess shouted as they drew closer.

'We could ask you the same question!' Anna retorted. 'Why's that worm drilling into the Apple of Liberty? Is it trying to find something?'

'None of your business,' said the Princess.

'Don't get any closer. I wouldn't like my assistants to harm you.'

Anna looked at Holly. In the mysterious way that sisters sometimes have of understanding one another without speaking, they agreed to jump on to the Princess's boat in three (nod), two (nod), one –

But Pepino jumped first!

And attacked the Princess's assistants!

SPLASH!

'Come on, Pepino!' Anna shouted.

PUNCH!

‘Well done, Peps!’ Holly yelled. ‘You’re a star!’

But though he fought valiantly, he was no match for the Easter Princess.

'Got you,' said the Princess. 'Pepino darling, I like you very much, but I need to finish what I started.'

The worm emerged again from the hole.

'Found it?' the Princess asked.

The worm nodded its head, opened its mouth …

And dropped something into the Easter Princess's hands.

'A gold nugget?' Holly mused. 'They dug into the Apple for *that*?'

'It must be worth more than it seems,' said

Anna. 'Come on, let's stop her!'

They jumped from their turtles to the boat.

But too late! As if it had exploded from the gold nugget, a giant bubble opened around the Princess and Pepino – and lifted them off the boat into the air!

'Drop that nugget, Princess!' Anna screamed. 'Whatever it is, it's not yours!'

'And it looks dangerous,' Holly pointed out.

'It's not the Emperor's either!' the Princess laughed. 'And yes, it *is* dangerous! That's precisely why …'

She stopped talking and looked up at the sky. 'Uh-oh. Red, blue and white alert launched, apparently!' she groaned. 'It's time to get far away from here!'

Barely a minute later, everything around them had changed colour!

The sky was full of WHITE EAGLES.

The sea was full of BLUE WHALES.

RED BEAVERS in tight ranks were swimming across the bay from the land.

And SHINY FIREFLIES fluttered around like stars!

The eagles swarmed around the Easter Princess, talons out and the beavers were already building a gigantic dam of wood and earth around the Apple. In the sea, the whales began throwing jets of water at the Princess.

Anna and Holly jumped on the backs of two eagles. In a few seconds, they were close to the Easter Princess.

'Get out of my way!' the Princess yelled.

Pepino punched a fist through the gelatinous surface of the giant bubble and Holly reached out to grab it.

Suddenly a deafening noise rose from the waves. A red lobster-shaped submarine surfaced, piloted by the Empress of Americanada herself, a fleet of smaller crab vessels alongside.

'FIRE!' the Empress shouted. And a flurry of puffer fish shot out of the water towards the Apple.

'Hey!' Anna yelled, as the spiky fishes ricocheted around them.

'SEAWEED RIFLE!' the Empress ordered, and her army fired swathes of sticky seaweed.

'Auntie!' Pepino screamed. 'Stop! You'll hurt us!'

But the Empress didn't seem to care. 'EAGLES! ATTACK!'

The eagles dived towards the Easter Princess, launching their talons and beaks at her protective bubble. It slowly began to pull apart …

'Careful!' Holly yelled. 'We're here too!'

'WHALES! ATTACK!'

The whales doubled their efforts to pummel the bubble with streams of water – until the Princess dropped the nugget. It tumbled towards a rip in the bubble …

And *SPLASH!* It fell into the sea.

PLOF! A beaver dived after it and surfaced again, carrying it between its teeth.

'I'll have that, thank you very much,' said the Empress, then looking up at the disintegrating bubble, 'Quick, catch that Princess!'

Holly and Anna only just had time to save the falling Princess and the just-as-falling Pepino.

'Very good,' said the Empress, 'another victory. I like victories.'

'My, my, my! What's *happening* here?' boomed Charlus's amplified voice.

Charlus and Molly's hovercraft floated up to them. Further away, a boat carrying Emperor Sam and King Steve was approaching the island.

'What's going on?' Sam asked, disembarking. 'We've just finished baking. The pies are cooling down. Did you launch an alert?'

'The Easter Princess was trying to steal a gold nugget inside your Apple of Liberty, Uncle!'

Pepino shouted. 'But we stopped her!'

Emperor Sam turned very pale.

'What nugget?' King Steve asked.

'Oh, nothing,' said Emperor Sam.

'Americanada in danger! Emperor Sam's secret nugget stolen by enemy Princess!' Charlus yelled. 'Show it to the Filmcrews, Your Imperial Highness! What's it for?'

'Oh, nothing,' repeated Emperor Sam.

'Nothing,' the Easter Princess snarled. 'Apart from *all his power*!'

And she shook her head so that her mask fell off …

Revealing a face that looked rather familiar.

Chapter Twelve

'*Sharon!*'

Emperor Sam and King Steve were dumbfounded.

'*Sharon!*' Steve repeated. 'Sharon, our little sister!'

'BREAKING NOOZE!' Charlus yelled hysterically. 'EASTER PRINCESS IS LONG-LOST "LOSER SISTER"!'

'Sharon,' King Steve sobbed, 'my darling sister! We thought you'd run away for ever! We thought you might have died!'

'I haven't,' said the Easter Princess. 'I was waiting for the right time for *revenge*.'

'Revenge!' Molly exclaimed. 'We love a good story of revenge. Don't we, Your Imperial Highness?'

'No, we don't,' grumbled Emperor Sam. 'Well, not this one, at least.'

'Oh, do tell us,' Anna said. 'We'd be *very* interested to hear your story ...'

The Filmcrews, a bit puzzled at first, split into two groups – one fluttering around Emperor Sam, and the other flocking around the returned Princess.

'Steve,' said the Easter Princess, 'wouldn't you agree that Emperor Sam was the worst brother ever?'

'Absolutely,' said King Steve. 'He was the most rubbish brother anyone could have nightmared of.'

'Wouldn't you agree, though, that he was also the cleverest, the most handsome, the most successful and the best liked?'

'He was indeed!' the King roared. 'The pompous brat!'

'Well,' said the Easter Princess, '*I know why*. I know where his eerie talents come from. I always knew!'

'They didn't come from anywhere!' quavered Emperor Sam. 'I was *born* with them!'

'Oh, no, he wasn't,' the Princess snarled. 'I read his secret diary, once, when we were children –'

'That's extremely bad of you!' Emperor Sam said.

'And I stole a page!' the Princess boomed. 'Look into my pocket, please, Pepino.'

'Yes, Auntie Sharon,' said Pepino, picking up a piece of paper in the Princess's pocket. Filmcrews gathered hungrily around the torn-out page.

Dear Diary,

Today my fairy godmother came by for my birthday. I was ALL FURIOUS because she gave me rubbish gifts like:

- A baby camel. IT STINKS and also SPITS.

- A flying broomstick. It HURTS my BUM.

- A little DEMON FROM HELL. That one is cool. I'll ask him to burn Steve's hair during the night.

But on the whole I was ~~dispoint~~ ~~diaspointe~~ ~~dissapoin~~ disappointed. So I did something VERY WRONG (but I don't care): I STOLE MY GODMOTHER'S MAGIC NUGGET.

It's a special fairy magic nugget. Now I'll be VERY POWERFUL and VERY HANDSOME and VERY CLEVER, not like Steve and Sharon who are ugly dunces.

'Oh, boy,' Charlus whispered. 'You mean to say that Emperor Sam –'

'*Stole* his power, yes!' the Easter Princess snapped. 'And, later on, he hid it in the Apple of Liberty to prevent anyone else from harnessing it! He knew that I had this piece of paper, so he forced me to leave Britland. But I vowed I'd be back!'

An '*Oh!!!*' of shock shook the crowd of Filmcrews.

'Well, Americanada, Emperor Sam is not that amazing after all,' Charlus said half-heartedly.

'He is still *very dishy*,' Molly protested.

'These allegations are false!' the Emperor protested. 'Who saved Americanada from alien invasions three hundred and eight times? Who single-handedly built a caramel skyscraper? Who –'

'Thanks to the magic nugget, not to *you*!' Anna yelled.

'Does it make a difference?' Sam roared.

'If it makes no difference,' Holly remarked, 'you should share the nugget, so that everyone can have a little bit of the power. If you care about your people, you should give them power too.'

'Oh yes? And how am I supposed to do that?'

'Well,' said Anna, 'how about if you scraped that magic nugget on to the pies you're about to feed the volunteers? That way, each of them will swallow a little bit of it, and the magic will spread to each of their states.'

'Ridiculous,' the Emperor grunted.

'Not ridiculous at all, Your Imperial Highness,' Charlus whispered. 'Do it, and you'll be remembered as Emperor Sam, the Generous.

Don't do it, and you'll have a revolution.'

The Emperor pondered a moment and then managed a sorry smile. 'Dear Americanadians,' he said, turning to face the Filmcrews, 'I am sorry I misled you all. But we have important work to do now – opportunities to seize, problems to solve, security matters to face! And the nugget will help us all!'

Molly clapped: 'Our fabulous Emperor will share his power with his people!'

The thunderous cheer and applause could be heard all the way from the city.

'That's a bit rich,' King Steve commented. 'He's just been revealed to be a fraud and everyone cheers him!'

'It's Americanada,' said Charlus. 'Everyone gets a second chance!'

'Do I get a second chance too?' asked the Easter Princess. 'Can I be free?'

'Of course, dearest sister,' said King Steve. 'Come with me to Britland. I'll make you Queen of the Tragically Unpeopled Island of Wight.'

'Erm,' said the Princess, 'no, thank you,

brother. I'd rather go back to my sunny island. I'm happy there.'

She hugged Holly, Anna, Pepino and King Steve, and shook Emperor Sam's hand. 'I hope you lose, though,' she whispered to Sam.

'Let the tasting begin!' Molly exclaimed. 'Time to see which brother is the best apple pie baker!'

Everyone crossed the bay again to go back to the studio, where the judges were waiting, blindfolded, near the two apple pies. The

Filmcrews zoomed in on their mouths as chunks of pie were spoon-fed to them.

'They don't know which one they're tasting!' Charlus yelled. 'Is it Emperor Sam's doubly delicious pie, or his brother's basic one? They seem to be enjoying both!'

Indeed, the volunteers didn't look unhappy to eat the glistening, sugary, juicy bits of pie, especially as each new spoonful was also sprinkled with magic nugget.

'Each of the judges will now write on paper whether they preferred the first or the second pie!' Charlus screamed. 'And we'll know the results in three minutes! ...'

'Two minutes! …'

'One minute! …'

'Well, after the advert break, of course.'

Chapter Thirteen

☆SHOX NEWS!☆

'NATION INCREDULOUS AS "LOSER BROTHER" KING STEVE OF TINY BRITLAND WINS FINAL OF ROYAL BAKE OFF'

'He did it, Mummy!' Pepino yelled to Queen Sheila on the phone. 'He won the final!'

'That's excellent,' said the Queen, 'I'll fire the chef. Steve can just cook for us from now on.'

Emperor Sam was a shadow of the man he'd once been.

'Congratulations, little brother,' he whispered to King Steve. 'Good for you that we picked judges with no taste.'

'What fair play,' Anna laughed. 'Can we get our prize now? You said we'd earn money for taking part in the contest.'

'I haven't got much cash on me,' said Emperor Sam, 'but have that small change.'

And he dumped a huge pile of banknotes on to Pepino's crown.

'Two hundred million dollars!' Holly marvelled. 'How much is that in Britlander pounds?'

'Two thousand,' said King Steve.

Pepino's eyes lit up. 'Just enough for –'

'The Holy Moly Holiday!' Anna and Holly shouted. '*Finally*, we've got enough money to go on the Holy Moly Holiday!'

'But first,' said King Steve, 'we've got to get home.'

'Oh, no,' Anna sighed. 'By Kryin'Air again?'

'No,' said the King. 'Sam mentioned that he was lending us a boat this time. It shouldn't be as tiring …'

Have you read Holly, Anna and Pepino's first two hilarious adventures?

OUT NOW

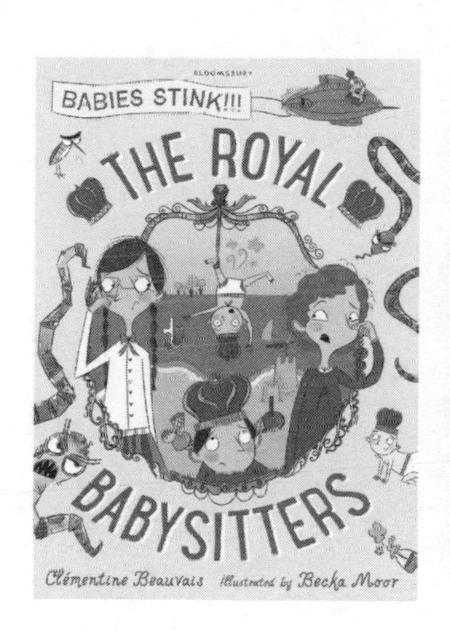

Join Holly, Anna and Pepino
on their fourth adventure,

THE VERY ROYAL HOLIDAY

Coming May 2016